JOE SAVES FLORIDA
and other adventures

By Ashna Dua

First published in 2020 by

Becomeshakespeare.com

One Point Six Technologies Pvt Ltd.
119-123, 1st Floor, Building J2, B - Wing,
WadalaTruck Terminal, Wadala East, Mumbai,
Maharashtra, India, 400022.
T: +91 8080226699

ISBN - 978-93-90463-35-0

Note from the author's desk

I am a ninth grader and I started writing this book in my third grade. A lot of the chapters in this book have been rewritten multiple times and I stopped writing about Joe for a few years due to a severe case of writer's cramps and a lack of inspiration. I even erased a few of Joe's adventures after he had already experienced them (sorry about that. Unfortunately, you will never know of those adventures of Joe!)

What's more, a few of the chosen saviours and a few other characters were even killed because of this and darling Joe was unable to look for a job like what us pitiful humans have to do... ☹ (I actually even had a chapter of Joe looking for a job, which was later deleted).

I enjoy playing the guitar, I am a brown belt in karate and I love to read fiction books about all sorts of things. I have forever got my head in the clouds and I tend to drift off while just staring into space. Sometimes, this gets me into a lot of trouble with my teachers (more like always!☺).

Anyways, just read about Joe and imagine his adventures in your head like they were your own... Enjoy!

Lots of love,

Ashna

For more information on the author, please visit www.ashnadua.com, and if you wish to contact the author, she will be available at ashna@ashnadua.com

Contents

Chapter 1

The Chosen Saviours

This is a story about a boy named Joe, who used to love the night. In his sleep he would dream about becoming a superhero.

But little did he know, what happened to him would be better than his best dream!

It was an ordinary day. Joe came home from school, made himself a snack and left for his tennis class — as usual. After his tennis class he came home tired, ate dinner and went to sleep. He had no clue that it would be the last time he would sleep in that bed.

He woke up suddenly in the middle of the night. Wondering what woke him up, Joe rubbed his eyes and looked around his room. Just then he spotted a cute little squirrel sitting by his bed.

Joe was startled! He looked at the clock, it was quarter to midnight. He looked out of the window, it was dark. He then looked back at the squirrel.

"Hello, Joe" said the squirrel. "My name is Tubby."

Joe was shocked. Not only was there a squirrel in his room but also it was a talking squirrel!

Let me introduce myself. I am the helper and advisor of the "Chosen Saviours".

Joe stared at the squirrel. He couldn't believe what he was seeing and hearing. He thought he was still dreaming. And he just threw himself on his pillow with a smirk on his face as to what a ridiculous dream this was.

The squirrel then jumped onto his pillow and whispered in his ear. "Helloooooooo Joe".

Joe woke up with a startle again and fell off his bed seeing the squirrel right next to him. He dragged himself behind on the floor scared and confused.

"What! Hmmm I mean who are you?" "Are you really talking? Talking to me? Or am I hearing things? Am I going crazy? What is happening to me?" Joe was full of questions and couldn't understand what was happening.

The squirrel smiled and softly spoke again. "Yes Joe. It's me talking to you. Don't be afraid, I'm a friend." Joe calmed down, still trying to fathom what had just happened.

"I am Tubby" continued the squirrel, "and I am the helper and advisor of the Chosen Saviours. Do you know about the Chosen Saviours my friend?"

Joe was still shaken but he gathered courage and slowly said, "No. I do not know about any saviours. But why are you in my room in the middle of the night?"

Tubby, the squirrel continued, "You have been selected as a member in the team of the Chosen Saviours. I had to come in the middle of the night because I did not want your parents to see me."

"Now let me explain to you what a saviour is. A saviour is someone who saves the World. Almost like a superhero. But unlike superheroes we don't have superpowers. We use our brains, our smartness, practical thinking skills and gadgets to solve human problems and problems in this World."

Joe was taken aback! Him?! A Saviour?! He still couldn't believe it. He thought this was some kind of a prank played on him by someone.

"WHY ME?!" he almost yelled. "Why not my friends or my cousins?"

"Because Joe, God chose *you* and not someone else. Because God saw good qualities in *you*, not in someone else. That is why *you* were chosen not someone else" replied Tubby.

Joe still had a lot of questions running in his head, and as he was thinking he blurted out, "What qualities? Stop fooling around with me whoever you are. I don't believe you"

Tubby stood quietly thinking of how he can make Joe believe he was telling the truth.

"I am telling the truth Joe, please believe me. I am not joking with you. You have really been chosen by God for your supreme qualities. Which qualities, I cannot answer as I am only the messenger." He paused to understand if Joe was listening and believing him. "I hope that as we get to know each other more, both of us will find out why God chose you. Just remember this, in order to be a good saviour you need to be true to yourself and always do the right thing even when the wrong thing is easier and more appealing" Tubby continued solemnly but with a small smile.

"I know all this may be difficult for you to understand and accept as it is all new to you. But please be patient and believe in me, I only want the best for you and protect you my friend".

"Are there others like me? How many and where do they live if there are? Are there any of my friends?" Joe asked, now curious to know more.

Tubby laughed. "So many questions! Are you always like this?" he asked, taking Joe's hand.

"All of the saviours live in the Land of Saviours" he said. "You must come there with me and see it for yourself" he added, tugging at Joe's wrist.

Joe's curiosity got the better of him, and he followed Tubby out of his room, and onto the lawn outside their house.

On the lawn was a large transparent ball big enough for a man and his team to step in. It had a control panel with handles and buttons on one side, and five red seats on the other. There was also a telescope to see far away objects coming towards you. Next to the controls there was a tiny screen which displayed the time it would take to reach your destination. Behind the ball was a little pipe.

"The Land of Saviours is located on top of the clouds. We're going to get there in a Transbocraft" said Tubby, pointing to the large ball.

Joe and Tubby stepped in, and Joe strapped himself into one of the red seats. He was looking around and before he knew it, they were in the air!

"How is it that this Transbocraft was not noticed by any of my neighbours when it was parked in my lawn? And what kind of a name is a Transbocraft anyway?" asked Joe. "The transbocraft is invisible to humans who are not saviours that's why" said Tubby, looking at Joe's curious face. "Trans for transport, bo for ball and craft for space-craft —that's how it gets its name. The transbocraft is an extremely fast and environment friendly vehicle. It travels 700.9 km per minute."

"How?" asked Joe. "It must need fuel, and a lot of fuel!"

"Not at all. The saviours make sure none of their devices or vehicles can harm humans. The transbocraft uses dried leaves to function. See that box?" said Tubby, pointing to a box with the words "1 KILOGRAM" written on top of it. "This box converts the leaves into oxygen, which comes out of the pipe you saw outside. This pushes the transbocraft ahead. One dry leaf takes the transbocraft ahead by 1 km."

Just as Tubby finished talking, they could view the Land of Saviours in a distance — in just fifteen minutes! The transbocraft landed on its landing pad and the door automatically opened. As Joe and Tubby walked out, Joe got his first view of the land. He was overwhelmed!

It was beautiful, with huge open grounds. In the open grounds strong men were training other kids like Joe. The grounds were surrounded by bushes with bright flowers. There were also toadstool houses all around in bright colours —green, red, yellow and more with a huge blue swimming pool. In the distance he could see huge willow trees. As they walked to one of the grounds, Joe noticed a big and beautiful rosebush. On it grew roses of different colours —yellow, red, pink, blue, white, orange —even black! It was surrounded by five glorious fountains —each spouting water of a different colour. The whole place had a beautiful mysterious pink glow, the air smelled of honeysuckle with Dandelion seeds all around. It felt like a magical place with all the unimaginably beautiful things picked from nature giving out vibes of calm and purity.

"Each group of saviours has its own colour. Blue is for the Super Saviours, yellow is for the War Breakers, greens are Guardians of the Galaxy, the Chosen Saviours are red and The Rescuers orange" said Tubby interrupting his thoughts.

Tubby took Joe to his group —the Chosen Saviours, who were sitting in one of the grounds. Tubby addressed them by saying, "Hello Chosen Saviours! This is your newest member and friend, Joe. Let's make him comfortable please. Why don't you introduce yourselves to him, my dear saviours."

"Hi, I am Sara. I am ten years old and I'm from Germany" said a short, petite girl who looked like she had a smart head. Her eyes sparkled like she was analysing everything she saw. "This is my brother Tim, he is eleven years old. Schön dich kennenzulernen Joe".

"Nice to meet you Joe is what she is saying" Tubby translated for those who did not understand German including Joe. While Tim raised his hand and waved a hello to Joe with a smile on his face.

"G'day mate. How ya doin? Nice to meet ya" said a girl with long brown hair and a thick accent. "I'm Jenny, from Australia and I absolutely love horses, do you like horses mate?"

Joe was taken by surprise and blurted out saying, "No. I mean yes of course I like horses."

"How do all of you speak English so fluently?" Joe asked.

"We have a very thorough English class here" replied Tim, smiling.

Another nice-looking boy with black hair and bright eyes came up to Joe and introduced himself. "Ola Joe. I'm Andrew. I come from Spain and I love animals. I am eleven years old and I go to Mongreyomentry School. Here, meet Fluffy" he said, taking a hamster out of his pocket. Joe stroked the little rodent's head with his finger.

"I am Jacob and I am eleven. I go to Marymount International School in Italy". Came a voice from behind. A slim tall boy with black straight hair and a very noticeable accent.

Joe noticed a boy walking towards them. He was looking down muttering under his breath in what Joe recognized as French. The boy looked up at Joe, and both exclaimed at the same time.

"Mathew!!"

"Joe!!"

Joe turned towards the other chosen saviours and said, "Mathew and I are best friends" beaming with happiness.

"We are neighbours too and go to the same school as well" added Mathew who was now beaming with joy.

"We go to Jr. Montersing International School and are both eleven years" added Joe, with his arm around Mathew's shoulder smiling at him and the other saviours.

As they all got busy chit chatting amongst themselves, Mathew pointed out something none of the others had noticed. "When we left Earth, it was night-time but over here the sun is rising. And my wrist watch is not working, it just stopped." Everyone else gave it a thought, agreed with his observation and went right back to chatting amongst themselves.

"Okay saviours, time for your first session" announced Tubby

"First session?!" yelled out Tim.

"Yes, of course, you are here to learn to be a saviour. There will be training sessions for that!" Tubby responded. "Here, meet your first trainer Mr. Brown"

Mr. Brown was a big built man with a deep voice. He had small eyes and a little long brown ruffled hair. "Hello Saviours. My name is Robert Brown but you can call me Mr Brown. I will teach you everything you need to know to help humans solve their problems." The Chosen Saviours looked at him with big eyes, almost trying to read him. "You might feel a little out of place now. That's okay" he said, looking at their expressions. "I too felt the same when I came here at first as a child."

The Chosen Saviours stared at him in confusion.

"If you had come here when you were a child, why didn't you go home after saving the World?" asked Jenny

Mr Brown laughed and said, "Once you come to the Land of Saviours, THIS becomes your home. You are the privileged few who are responsible for ridding our World of problems. Even though you will miss your parents and your home, you will also experience this place to be no less than home and all of us, a family. You will realise this needs to be done for the greater good." He ended with a smile and a sigh.

This shocked and scared everyone. They thought they were there only temporarily. Now they would never see their parents again! Everyone started crying. They wanted to go back home!

Mr Brown and Tubby tried to calm them down. "Don't you want to help save your own parents? If you cry then you won't be able to train and learn. If you don't learn then you can't help your family and friends. Be brave my dear Saviours." Said Mr. Brown with a feeling of empathy for them as he too felt the same pain as they felt today.

This seemed to take everyone's mind off their worries and focus on trying to save their families.

They started their session for the day.

They learned the various functions and understood the control panel of the transbocraft. They were taught to drive the transbocraft and how to be stealthy. They also learned about the special gadgets they had access to using and how to use 'Soogle' —the saviours' search engine.

Mr Brown shared tips and tricks and methods used to investigate and solve mysteries. After a full day's training with Mr Brown they took a liking for him and realised he was much warmer as a person than he comes across as.

It was dinner time and the sky had turned a beautiful pink and orange. Mr Brown led the chosen saviours to a dining hall. It was inside a willow tree where a delicious meal awaited them. The aroma of the food made Joe even hungrier. He looked around and saw a huge dining area with long tables and benches to sit on either side. The ceilings had beautiful red chandeliers lit up and hanging down. There were paintings of some people all over the walls that Joe didn't recognise.

As they walked closer, Joe noticed everyone standing patiently in line with their plates in hand to serve themselves from the food counter. There was no person serving, everyone had to serve themselves and then go and sit on the bench to eat their meal. Everyone was smiling and laughing and talking to each other, nobody was grumpy or sad or even upset with one another. He suddenly felt a lot of love within him and a feeling of belonging to this new family. Joe could not believe that the food was his favourite—pork chops, fried rice and ice cream sundae for dessert. "I could get used to living without mom and dad, if I get to eat this kind of food every day AND be a superhero!" thought Joe. He quickly ate his dinner as he was starving.

Once everyone had finished dinner, Joe saw some of them clearing the tables, stacking the used plates on a separate counter and picking up food dropped on the floor. Everyone had to do their own work, manage and care for the place together, saviours and teachers alike. There was no difference between anyone, they were all equal.

Joe and his friends were then taken to another building. It was huge with high ceilings and dim lighting all over. It was a beautiful dormitory. It had lime green walls and large comfortable beds with bright blue sheets. Over each bed was a plate bearing a saviour's name with a small cabinet next to it to keep their clothes in. Joe walked around looking for his bed, threw himself on it and shut his eyes at once, tired after an exhausting and adventurous day.

Chapter 2

Joe's First Adventure

11:00pm
12:00
1:00am
2:00am
2:01am
2:05am

"Ugh! I can't sleep!" Joe exclaimed in annoyance. He kept thinking about his loving mother and strict but warm father. He thought about his friends. He even felt an unexpected affection and longing for his school!

'I'm thinking about school back at home and am actually missing it!' Joe mused amused. 'Wait, not home. THIS is home now.' And, in a weird sort of way, it was. 'I'll go visit mom and dad often though.' Comforted for now, tired from his long day and deep thinking, Joe collapsed on his bed and fell asleep.

A loud noise awoke Joe the next morning. He, along with Andrew and Mathew, raced out to see what was happening. Sara ran towards them screaming, "Huge ugly trolls and monsters are invading Florida!!" Joe was stunned! Florida was his state! It needed to be saved!

Just then Tubby walked towards them, looking grave. "Saviours, gather here please. This would be a good time to test what you've learnt" he said looking at their grim and now shocked faces. It had only been a day since Joe had joined the saviours. "I know it may be a little too soon for you Joe, to be out on a mission right now, but we need you at this time of threat, Florida needs you to save it." He added looking right at Joe and the others. "Do you accept this mission my brave saviours?"

"YES!" they shouted in unison.

The chosen saviours sprang into action, dressing up, packing their gear and piling it into their transbocraft to descend to Earth. They all sat down quickly and quietly. Every single one of their hearts were racing and they were worried. Very worried. Of what? Of failing. Of something going wrong. Of losing one of their members and soon becoming friends.

On their way, they ran out of fuel. The transbocraft stopped in mid- air and just stood still. Thankfully, there was always a can of spare dried leaves in the transbocraft's storage cupboard.

"I'll get the fuel." Said Sarah as she was closest to the cupboard.

"This is a bad omen for sure." Cried Matthew who had always been believing of things like this very much.

"Matt stop. You're going to jinx us if you say stuff like that." Snapped Joe, irate.

When they finally reached earth, they landed in a vast forest in Jacksonville, Joe's home-city. This surprised Joe as he wasn't aware of any forests around Jacksonville, certainly not ones with such big tall trees. Also, this forest seemed very different from any others that he had seen. Creepy grey washing machines that could fit a grown man were placed behind these trees.

Strange machines in the forest

(Joe's first adventure)

Something was off, he didn't know what exactly but it didn't feel right. That's when he remembered the first thing that they had learnt in their class the day before.

Mr Brown had taught them as a part of their training, never to touch an unknown thing so they avoided the machines, but instead went around them. They needed to help each other sometimes. Joe needed help around an especially large machine.

"Hurry up" said Jacob to Tim, who was helping Joe. "I can hear something coming"

As Tim tried to hurry, he let go of Joe's hand and Joe fell right into the machine.

Everyone watched in horror as the machine started pulling out Joe's teeth to make them longer and his face churned and changed. Joe too seemed to be in a lot of pain. When he was out of the machine, the other saviours were horrified. However, Joe was plain relieved, until he realised that he now looked like a vampire!

"Nooooooooo!!" he screamed with tears streaming down his cheeks, frightening the others, who quickly ran away.

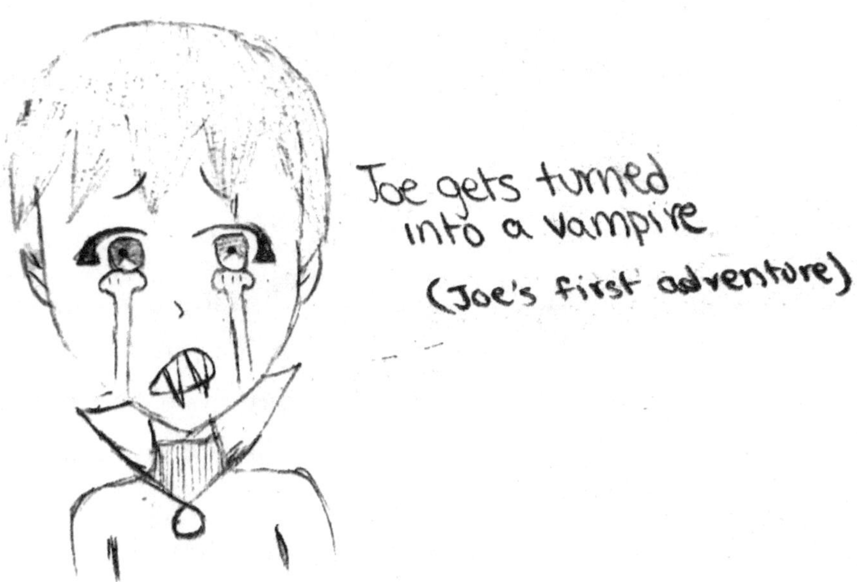

Joe too was scared, but realized quickly that even though he looked like a vampire now, he was still a human and saviour on the inside.

"I told you that something bad would happen! It was a bad omen before!" Mathew screamed. This time no one refuted his words. Jenny just sighed in defeat.

Terrified after what had happened to Joe, the chosen saviours abandoned the mission and Joe and went home to their Land. Joe couldn't tell them that he was still himself. But he was not going to give up like the others. He continued his journey as a vampire, dodging the machines and made his way to the city where he found trolls and monsters terrifying everyone. Humans were running helter-skelter, trying not to be eaten by the trolls. Joe imagined his own mom and dad being eaten but he just couldn't. He had to save everyone!

Joe used Soogle to find out everything about trolls and monsters. He learnt that trolls melt when you pour hot water on them, even if it is very little, and that monsters die when you pull their tails.

He also learnt that the monsters like to invade big and tall buildings. This gave Joe an idea. He made his way to the city centre that contained all the high-rises. Once there, he went to the Hillman Industries, the largest and tallest building in the city. It was full of filthy monsters. He went in quietly and pulled one monster's tail. The monster died with a loud POP. This alerted the other monsters and they saw Joe. The monsters tried to fight Joe but Joe shot arrows at them with his Saviour's watch. They fell, Joe pulled their tails and POP went the monsters!

Once all the monsters in Hillman Industries were dead, he decided to move to the next part of the plan. For that, he needed to go to his house.

He reached home and rang the bell. His mom opened the door.

"Hi mom, can you help me please?" he asked

His mom looked terrified of Joe's vampire appearance. Joe realized that, smiled and showed her his birthmark on the shoulder. She still had a tough time recognising him. After a little more convincing she finally trusted him. She had a lot of questions for Joe. But Joe did not have the time. He had to take care of the trolls.

He went in, boiled a lot of water and carried it out in buckets. He turned on his special rocket-launcher shoes, flew up into the sky carrying the large buckets and turned in a 360° circle to view the situation.

The trolls varied in height—from between 5 feet to 8 feet. They were green and had boils all over their bodies. Their large, yellow eyes surveyed their prey as they lumbered around on their big and wonky feet.

Joe looked at all the bodies littered on the road and decided to end this. He spilt the hot water all over the trolls. They all died immediately. When all the trolls were dead, he went back to the transbocraft and flew to the Land of Saviours.

On reaching the Land of Saviours, Joe found Tubby waiting for him. The Chosen Saviours had already received a huge scolding from Tubby and Mr Brown for having left Joe behind. Tubby was shocked at Joe's vampire appearance but was equally delighted to see Joe back. He felt responsible for Joe because after all it was he who had brought Joe to the Land of Saviours!

"I am proud of you Joe" he said. "You saved Florida all by yourself! I think you are now capable enough to graduate to the stage where you do not need helpers or advisors. You can be on your own."

'Congratulations Joe!' said the other saviours. "We are sorry we left you behind" added Sara, "we were just too scared and defeated."

Joe was happy and excited by what Tubby had said. He could now leave the Land of Saviours or move around without asking anyone. He was presented with some gadgets to survive in case of emergencies and most importantly —a stealth suit. Joe now had the whole kit and all the tools required to save the world when the need arises.

Everyone was grateful for the good work Joe had done, and yet they were uncomfortable around him because of his vampire appearance. Joe realised that others did not like that he now looked like a vampire. He decided to leave the Land of Saviours.

He packed, said goodbye to everyone and went to live alone in a cloud palace, high up in the clouds. He was told by everyone that he was welcome to come back at any time. But as long as he could help people, Joe didn't care where he stayed, or what he looked like.

Chapter 3

Joe's Super-'Savage' Adventure

Joe was having the delicious tuna sandwich he had been craving, in his cloud palace when his trouble thermometer picked up trouble in Kenya, in the famous Nairobi National Park. He set off immediately in his transbocraft to investigate the matter.

At first, the National Park rangers and officers were scared of him. After all, he did look exactly like a vampire. After convincing them that he wasn't dangerous, they told him that the animals had turned extremely ferocious —like never before! They had become overly aggressive —growling, snarling and trying to bite everyone —even the rangers who fed them! Plus, their eyes had turned red.

Joe saw a cute, red squirrel that looked pretty ordinary. It seemed harmless but the moment Joe went near it, the squirrel bit Joe's shoe and snarled at him. Joe retreated quickly.

The squirrel reminded Joe of Tubby. He remembered what Tubby said to him on the first night when they met —that he was the chosen saviours' adviser and helper. Joe sent Tubby a message with his watch, asking for his help on this case. Tubby replied, "This could be a disease!"

Joe had to find a way to stop the infection, and find an antidote to cure the ones already infected. But he was a saviour, not a doctor! He couldn't do this by himself. He needed help. He made a report about the happenings and then went to the biggest and most knowledgeable scientist and veterinarian in the land of saviours Dr Fredrickson Malory.

Dr Malory and Joe had met at the land of saviours. Though Dr Malory was a trainer like Mr. Brown, he had left the Land of Saviours to help humankind as a doctor. Joe left immediately to see him.

Dr Mallory was happy to meet Joe. "I have heard so much about you!" he said.

"You have? But I am only a beginner." Joe asked, confused.

"Of course I know about you! Everyone does. You fought the trolls all by yourself —even though one of the machines laid by the trolls turned you into a vampire"

Joe beamed, but immediately came back to the problem at hand. He told the doctor about the animals going savage.

Dr Mallory listened to Joe's report. "It appears to be caused by some sort of disease like jaundice," he said, scratching his beard.

"Can you make an antidote?" asked Joe

Before the doctor could answer, there was a small buzz, and each received a notification on his watch —Saviours' Leader— Choosing Ceremony Day After! Both of them looked at each other in surprise!

As is clear by its name, the leader choosing ceremony was a ceremony to choose the leader of the saviours. Each group of saviours has their own leader, but they all need someone who will keep them from going astray and rebelling. Someone to keep peace and the spirit of unity. The best part, Joe had been nominated this time even though he had only completed one mission. Joe thought about how exhilarating it would be to be the leader but that was when he realized that he had a problem on hand.

Then Joe came back to the subject and asked Dr Fredrickson about the antidote.

"It is difficult, as it is a rare disease, but I will definitely try for you." said Dr Mallory

"That would be great Doctor – if anyone can do it, it is only you" said Joe

Dr. Mallory seemed flattered. "I'll do it, but on one condition," he said.

"What is that?"

"You must vote for me tonight —at the Leader-Choosing Ceremony. Of course, I will vote for you too!"

"Oh definitely" said Joe, and they both laughed heartily. It was clearly meant to be a joke but Joe was determined to vote for Fredrickson Malory if he could find a cure for the problem that was threatening humans and animals alike. Animals for obvious reasons and humans because they were the ones getting terrorized by the poor, infected animals.

After a little more small talk, Joe realized that he was holding up the work to find the antidote. He decided to leave as he wanted to give Malory his space to work.

After Joe left, Dr Fredrickson got to work immediately. He made many concoctions but none served his purpose. They were of all colours and serve all sorts of purposes but the one needed. Fredrickson made more inventions in 24 hours than he had in 2 years! One of those inventions even burnt off his eyebrows!

He worked straight for 32 hours and at last, hit the jackpot! He called and informed Joe immediately.

Joe was ecstatic to hear the news, but now they had a different problem in front of them. They had no time to lose —the 'Jaundice' had spread all over Kenya. How was Joe going to administer the antidote to all the animals at the same time?

He searched in his pack of devices and found something interesting. It was called an All-Around Vaccine. It was a peculiar looking bottle with an atomiser and a keypad. Once the bottle was filled with the antidote, Joe simply had to type a name on the keypad, and the atomiser would spray it on that person or object. Joe was confused at first, but after discussing it with Tubby, Joe decided that this was the object that would help him cure the animals. He typed in the term 'Infected animals' onto the keypad and spread the invention all around. He used this nifty device to cure all the affected wild animals in Kenya at the same time. And within hours, all the animals came back to their usual behaviour.

His job done, Joe flew back to the Land of Saviours for the Leader-Choosing ceremony. There were discussions and talks of who should be chosen as the leader and the kind of qualities a leader should possess. Then, everyone was given a sheet of paper and asked to write the name of their chosen person and drop it in a big box. There was a lot of tension and excitement in the air.

Once the voting was done, the counting process began. After a couple of hours, it was time for the announcement and Tubby was seen on stage holding the microphone. He announced that the new leader was: JOE!!!!

"In a very short time Joe, you have become popular with the other saviours, have bravely tackled your very first mission on your own, and even though you look like a vampire, you continue to help people and animals alike. We know that you have only completed two missions but you have done them with such skill and determination that we want to learn from and with you. We'll explore together should you choose to accept this position." said Tubby, as all the others listened and cheered.

Joe felt humbled and honoured to be chosen as the leader of all the saviours. He could hardly believe it! He was now given a phone via which he could supervise training of all the saviours. He could overlook missions and call any of the saviours or trainers from different groups to help him at anytime, anywhere in the world.

Chapter 4

Joe's Hi- Tech Mission

After becoming the leader of the saviours, Joe took on the job of protecting and looking after the world. He loved this job, even though it was a great responsibility, because he could now meet humans more often. He was also learning a lot more about the world and the different types of threats the world faced. Having gone on loads of missions, he had realized that the world needed a lot more safety precautions than the humans could afford to give themselves. To fulfil his job of protecting Earth, Joe took daily rounds of the world to check that everything was in order.

Once, while taking his daily rounds, he noticed something strange —humans seemed to be acting more and more like robots.

Joe took a few more rounds over the next few days and realized that technology was indeed slowly taking control of humans' minds!

People were walking, talking and doing things like robots — without any feelings or thoughts! They would soon turn completely insensitive, and become like machines! That would not be a good thing! Although machines are effective and important, if humans continued acting like robots, they would lose their creativity and emotions. Already, they were more interested in their gadgets than in each other. They rarely spoke and spent quality time together. The change of behaviour was very worrying.

Joe decided to observe this change for a few more days and then decide what to do about it. However, in the next week, Joe's worst fears came true! While taking his weekly round around the world, he saw that all the humans' bodies were slowly turning into robot bodies.

Joe made it his mission to save the humans, but he had to do it alone. The other saviours were humans too, and the machines could easily turn them into robots as well. Since he was now a vampire, the machines could not affect him.

Joe went home to pack and when he came back out he saw that not only were humans turning to robots, but computers and machines had come alive and were now controlling the world.

Joe knew he had to find a way to beat the machines. He searched Soogle for an answer. Joe found out that the only way to stop machines from taking over, was to kill their leader.

Once their leader was dead, slowly all the other computers and machines would stop working, humans would come back from their robot-like state and start controlling the machines and computers again.

The leader of the machines was called Mr Mobile. He lived in a highly guarded area, surrounded by very intelligent machines. This made killing him very difficult. Joe decided to dress up like a computer and seek a meeting with the leader. He made a computer-suit for himself that made him look exactly like one of the machines. It was made out of cardboard, metal and other materials.

Since machines had low sensitivity, they couldn't tell the difference between Joe and the other machines.

He told Mr. Mobile's guard that he was here to warn the leader about the 'Vampire—Saviour Joe' who was trying to destroy the machines. And it worked! No one could recognize him. He was easily allowed to enter Mr. Mobile's office. Now came the tough part – killing Mr. Mobile.

Mr Mobile was basically a huge mobile phone as tall as a human. He had eyes, a nose and mouth on his screen. He could bend his head. His leader was wearing a hat which was black in colour with a golden rim. He also had black shoes and a bowtie, which made him look like a kid.

Joe could not stop staring at Mr Mobile and sensing that, the leader became a little nervous, annoyed and suspicious.

"What have you come in for?" he growled. "Do you intend to say anything? Who are you?"

"I am one of your computers" blurted Joe, startled at hearing Mr. Mobile.

"Why are you here?"

"I have come to warn you. There is a Vampire—Saviour named Joe who is creating a lot of trouble for us. He is very annoying and is always showing up with his naïve ways, trying to get the humans back. We must do something about him."

Mr Mobile continued to look at Joe suspiciously. Joe realized he needed to win his trust.

"I came to you because you are the most intelligent of all machines. Only you can help catch this saviour" he said, trying to flatter Mr. Mobile.

Hearing this, Mr Mobile smiled.

Joe was relieved. "I have a plan here for how we can accomplish our objective." he said, taking out a piece of paper from inside his costume. Mr Mobile took the paper from Joe. As soon as he bent over to read it, Joe took out the taser that he was hiding inside his costume, and used it on the wires connecting Mr. Mobile to his charger. Due to the electric overload, Mr mobile died on the spot!

The other machines soon went into a panic and ran around trying to attack other humans and protect themselves. Joe knew he could not wait for them to get discharged automatically, he would have to kill them too. He armed himself with sleep darts, a self-filling water gun, a scissor and a sword. He spurted water all over the computers so they stopped working, cut their wires, slashed screens with his swords and shot sleep darts at the humans to keep them out of harm's way in the battle.

By now, the other saviours, along with Dr. Fredrickson Malory, Tubby and Mr Brown were here, fighting alongside Joe. The machines tried to fight, but with their leader dead they were running out of power and dying quickly. As each machine died, every human connected to them returned to their full human state again.

Having regained their humanity again, all the humans began assembling the dead computers and machines and rewiring them so that they couldn't ever take over the world again.

"It is because we became so much dependent on them, and forgot how to do things on our own, that they became so powerful," they told Joe and the other saviours.

"That's right!" said Tubby! "What humans can do —no other machine can —and we must always remember that!"

The humans agreed with Tubby and cheered for Joe and the saviours. Joe was not just the Saviours' leader now, he was also the leader of humans. The humans welcomed him to come and stay with them whenever and for as long as he liked. They loved him —— despite his vampire—like appearance!

Chapter 5

Joe's diary

7:30pm, 30th September 2019

Dear diary,

Today was so tiring. I am simply exhausted! I have been supervising the super—saviours' training the entire day —and they are still only learning the basics. I helped them learn faster by showing them a few tricks. They have become much better than they were in the morning.

I wish something exciting would happen—there are no missions, no adventures and no fun at all. Don't misunderstand me —I love being the leader of all saviours; it's just that I get so excited when there is a problem at hand. Not the kind of problems that hurt others —not even like my first mission. Just maybe —a tiny robbery? That would be fun. Uh oh, Tubby wants to talk to me about some strategy for the saviour games. They are happening next week. Got to go, be back soon.

8:45pm, 1st October 2019

Hi diary,

I'm back. Let me tell you more about the saviour games. It's not very different from the sports day we have in school. Different Saviour Teams are going to compete with each other. There are no particular rules —saviours can use their wits and tools to solve their problem in any way —as long as they don't sabotage the other teams. If they do sabotage other teams, they will be disqualified at once. The events are fun! There's fighting with various weapons, knot-tying competitions, treasure hunts, races, quizzes and riddles. I can't compete, since I am the leader. But I get to judge and choose who will be given the All-Stars Saviour Award. I really want the Chosen Saviours' Team to win, but I can't be helping them. If they win, then it has to be because of their own hard work. I was chosen as the leader to be fair and not partial so I will do so, even if it means that my team won't win. It is late now and I should sleep because I have to be fresh tomorrow to check all the other teams' practice sessions. Goodnight.

9:00pm, 2nd October 2019

Dear diary,

It is an emergency! Tim woke me up to tell me that the Chosen Saviours' practice equipment is missing. Without the equipment they simply won't be ready in time for the Games. I spoke to everyone and I think that this is a case of sabotage. One of the other teams is trying to prevent the chosen saviours from winning. But which one can it be? Not the Super Saviours surely. Could it be the Guardians of the Galaxy? Or maybe it is The Rescuers —or the War Breakers. I don't know. I'm very upset.

Everyone knows that teams who cheat will be disqualified. This is very unlike Saviours. After all the motto of the saviour games is "Win fairly with pride, or lose to try harder next time". I must go to help the others, solve the case. After all, it is my duty as the leader. I will write as soon as I find out something. Bye!

10:00pm, 3rd October 2019

Dear diary,

I have been searching for the missing equipment the whole day and just some time ago I found it stuffed in a corner of the garbage, waste and broken materials closet. I wonder who did it. Hmm... Well, now I have a mystery to solve. My wish came true!! But I can barely keep my eyes open while writing all of this. Goodnight!! ☺

8:00pm, 4th October 2019

Dear diary,

I think that the Guardians of the Galaxy or the War Breakers are the culprits. I can't be sure yet, but when the missing equipment was found, they seemed crestfallen. More importantly – neither of these teams was practising when the equipment was stolen. Where were they? What were they up to? I questioned all the teams, and they all had rock—solid alibis —all except for these two. Still, this is just a guess, I need to investigate some more, because without evidence I can't do or say anything. IT IS JUST SO FRUSTRATING!!!!!!!!!!!!!! I MEAN LIKE REALLY! WHY WOULD SOMEONE WANT TO HURT ANOTHER TEAM? I know that I am screaming but I just can't believe that any of the saviours will do something as un-heroic as this. It is getting late, I think I should go to investigate and find proof. Bye diary, I will let you know when I find out who is the thief and then they really will be punished.

7:00pm, 5th October 2019

Dear diary,

I finally found out who the thief is and I can't believe it! It was Andrew who did it and tried to sabotage his own team. I asked him why and guess what! He wanted the Chosen Saviours to lose!! His sister who is in The Rescuers mocked him, saying I would favour the Chosen Saviours – and Andrew didn't want everyone to think that —so he sabotaged his own team! I have never heard of anything like this! Andrew was feeling guilty so he told his sister Gabrielle who in turn told Mr Brown who told me. I was furious, but then I realized Andrew was not trying to hurt his team-mates out of spite. He simply didn't want the others to think I was favouring his team. Plus, Gabrielle asked me not to punish her brother and so I let the Chosen Saviours remain in the saviour games. They were all very happy, even Andrew. Gabrielle apologised to him and to me. Now can you believe it, the saviour games are tomorrow!

7:00pm, 6th October 2019

Dear diary,

The saviour games were very exciting, and guess who won it - Gabrielle's team- The Rescuers! She was so happy and so was Andrew as that meant that I was not at all partial to my own team. YAY!!! But don't think that I chose The Rescuers because of the teasing, they were really the best. And turns out that when I was interviewing the 5 teams, the Guardians of the Galaxy and the War Breakers wouldn't confess their alibis as they were having a secret party. They came and confessed after the Saviour Games were over. Since they were only having a bit of fun, I did not punish them. Other teams were expecting me to, because they were upset at being left out of the party – but I don't think having fun with your own team members is a crime. What a lot of excitement there has been over the past few days, phew! Now I can finally sleep peacefully! Bye and goodnight!

Chapter 6

The Broken Invention

Joe was visiting his good friend Frankenstein after many months. Frankenstein was a scientist, an inventor and was known as a 'Daredevil Maniac'.

Frankenstein did not have many friends because most people thought him to be a bit weird. That is the reason why Joe and Frankenstein were such good friends because Frankenstein had all the time in the world for his only friend —except when he was working on a new invention.

And that is exactly why he called Joe —to see his latest invention! He was very excited and so was Joe.

Frankenstein's house was just about as weird as he was. The door was olive green and the walls were black. On the inside, the house had one wall painted yellow, one purple, one red and one blue. The ceiling was grey while the entire floor was fuchsia. It was an ordeal to the eyes. Anyone who entered was immediately repulsed by all these colours that clashed with each other in the most terrible way.

Wanting to welcome his friend nicely, Frankenstein served Joe some tea and snacks when Joe had arrived. Frankenstein's taste in food was just as weird as his choice of colours. There were fish and chocolate flavoured cookies served with liquorice and lemongrass tea, peanut butter, jam and pickle sandwiches, Oreos covered with orange syrup, sausages dipped in Nutella, and fries with custard. Because of his peculiar brain Frankenstein made peculiar things. At times these things could turn out quite amazing, but Joe did not want to get sick just in case these particular snacks weren't and so he politely refused most of the items —and just sipped tea.

After the unusual tea Joe was ushered into a small lab. In the corner was a huge box. Frankenstein lifted the box and revealed what looked like a TV. "Behold the time machine C2 T.V 9952" he exclaimed!

Joe thought that his friend had finally gone truly crazy. The invention looked exactly like a television set to him —nothing else.

"Can this TV actually take a person back or forward in time?" he asked Frankenstein doubtfully.

"Not actually, but if you type an incident or a person and a particular year using this remote, this TV will show you back in time, just like a regular TV! Try it!"

Joe took the remote and typed '1964 + my grandfather'. On the screen appeared black and white events of Joe's grandfather joining the Indian Oil Corporation on 4th July, then celebrating Diwali with his grandmother and then travelling to a beautiful island on a ship. Joe was amazed! He had only seen them in photos, and he stood there mesmerised, looking at his grandparents. He was just about to type in something else in the remote when the TV started smoking.

Both looked at the machine in horror as dark black smoke billowed from it. It smelled foul and made them cough.

"There must be some (cough) problem (cough) with it" gasped Frankenstein as he turned off the machine's switch. "Why don't you (cough) go out and (cough) wait, while I (cough) fix this?" he choked and sputtered to Joe, while fiddling with the knobs on the machine.

By now, the room was engulfed in smoke. It smelled of rotten eggs and sour cheese mixed with onions. Joe was only too glad to leave.

"There's some dinner (cough cough) in the kitchen (cough) Help yourself" rasped Frankenstein, fiddling with the machine as Joe fled the lab.

Joe had not eaten anything at tea so he almost ran to the kitchen. To his dismay, dinner was just as weird as tea —salami with grapes, pepperoni pizza with chocolate sauce on top, hamburger with strawberry jelly, hot dogs with whipped cream and for dessert there were fish fingers with ice cream. But Joe was hungry, so he ate. Surprisingly, everything tasted quite okay.

Joe felt better after dinner. He wondered if he should check on Frankenstein, but curious noises were coming from the lab, and Joe remembered how bad the smell was, so he stayed in the kitchen, amusing himself with Frankenstein's gadgets.

After an hour and a half Frankenstein came back out and told Joe he had fixed it.

"Come take a look" he beamed.

"Are you sure the smell is gone?" asked Joe

"Of course" he replied, almost gleefully, pushing Joe towards the lab

As soon as Joe entered, there was a loud "pop" and the lights went out. An eerie sound made a chill run down Joe's spine. Joe turned to get out of the lab but the door was locked! "AAAHHHHHHH!!!!!!!!!! HHHHHEEEEEEELLLLLLLLPPPPP!!!!!" he screamed "I AAMM LLOOCCKKEEDD IINNSSIIDDEE!!!! Suddenly a light came on and there was Frankenstein, surrounded by all the other Chosen Saviours!

"SURPRISE!!!" they shouted, "Happy birthday Joe!"

Joe was in disbelief! Tubby, Sara, Tim, Jacob, Andrew, Mathew, Jenny, Jimmy —even Fredrickson Malory and Mr. Brown were standing before him, holding a large cake with many candles, balloons and gifts!.

Happy Birthday
Joe!
(The broken invention)

"Sorry to trick you Joe, but we knew you would have never agreed to a party for yourself, so we had to do this!" said Sara.

"So the machine..?" he looked at Frankenstein, puzzled.

"Not broken, just a little trick to distract you while we set everything up" said Frankenstein waving at all the beautiful streamers and bunting hanging from the ceiling!

Joe was amazed and very, very happy. "Now everyone" said Frankenstein playing music, "let's dance and eat! I have some delicious food here!"

Everyone stopped and stared at Frankenstein. "Oh don't worry, I haven't made it" he said, looking at their worried faces. "It's pizza that I ordered – just like you like it!"

Everyone laughed.

Joe had the most fabulous party ever!!! Everyone had fun!! They ate pizza, danced, sang, had drinks, gave gifts, played games and tried Frankenstein's invention— the C2 T.V. 9952.

Joe got the machine as a gift and loved his birthday. It was unforgettable —— better than any birthday he had celebrated on Earth.

Chapter 7
Joe Is In Trouble!

Joe paced about his room in a pensive mood. He was tense. He looked around and sighed. Though he was a leader, he wished he had someone to help ease his mind at this time. Joe thought of Jacob. He had not seen his friend from the Chosen Saviours in a very long time. Joe decided to write to him.

Dear Jacob,

I haven't met you in a long time. Please give me the pleasure of your company for tea tomorrow at 3pm.

I want to share with you some stories of my adventures and I also need your help.

I will be waiting for you at the following address,

House #31,

Lily Avenue,

Orlando,

Florida.

Please come at 3:00pm.

Your friend,

Joe

Joe mailed the letter via the Saviours' Super-Speed mailing service, ate his dinner and went to bed.

'The evil Super Saviours' trainer has escaped from Prison!!!' Jacob was just reading this on his saviour-screen when he received Joe's letter.

How wonderful! He thought to himself after reading the letter. And how terrible — he thought, looking at the news on the saviour-screen.

The next day found Joe preparing all kinds of delicious goodies. He baked scones, tea-cake, tarts, macaroons and gingerbread and set out jam, butter and fresh juice along with a steaming pot of tea for his friend.

At 3pm Jacob arrived at Joe's house to find a beautiful and tasty spread. They sat down to tea and talked about Joe's adventures and had a good time just like old times. Then Jacob remembered that Joe had asked for his help on something. He asked Joe what it was.

"Last week someone stole a lot of things from Tubby's house and everyone —— even Tubby— thinks it was me even though I am the leader!" he said, morosely.

Jacob was shocked! "Why does everyone think that it was you?" he asked.

"Tubby found my gloves in his house after the robbery. I need your help to prove I am innocent, otherwise I might not get to remain the leader anymore".

Jacob promised to help Joe and after the delicious treat they set off to the Land of Saviours.

Joe and Jacob received a very cold welcome at the Land of Saviours. People avoided Joe, or they stared at him, whispering to each other. No one greeted them like before. Jacob noticed this and both of them decided to go to the root of the matter. They went straight to Tubby.

Tubby seemed in a grumpy mood. He was not at all happy to see Joe. "Why don't you tell us exactly what happened that night" asked Jacob. Tubby huffed. "Why are you asking me this again when he already knows everything" he said, pointing to Joe and shutting the door in their faces.

Jacob was surprised. This seemed very unlike Tubby. He suggested that maybe they should go and visit their other friends— the rest of the Chosen Saviours while Tubby had some time to himself. Joe agreed.

On their way, they saw another one of the posters announcing the escape of the evil trainer from prison.

Super saviours' trainer wanted poster

(Joe is in trouble)

Joe wrinkled his nose. "I've heard that news" he said. "I have saviours on the lookout for him." The two of them continued to walk around searching for the others and eventually found them in the dorm room.

Joe asked them if they knew what happened that night, when Tubby got robbed. "I know!" Tim piped up most helpfully. "That night, Tubby was sleeping when he heard a noise. He woke up with an startle. When he looked around he found most of his belongings missing and his room in a mess. When he got out of bed, he stepped on something —a glove. He immediately recognized it as yours, Joe. He has since been telling everyone that you are a thief. That's all we know anyway" he shrugged. The others looked at Joe sadly.

"But that doesn't make sense" said Jacob, puzzled. "Tubby has such great faith in Joe. Even if Joe's glove was found in his room, why didn't he question Joe, before telling everyone he was a thief?"

Everyone looked at each other, nodding their heads. Jenny broke the silence. "Tubby has changed" she said. "He gets angry and is grumpy all the time. He is no longer friendly and is often mean. It is as if it is not him. Come to think of it, he has been this way since the past two weeks, even before the robbery."

"What are you saying?" asked Jacob.

"It's true" insisted Jenny, "We all think so." The others nodded along.

"What if Tubby is not tubby?" quipped Joe. "What if someone has taken the place of Tubby, someone who wants to get me in trouble?

Or what if Tubby is being forced to do it?"

Everyone looked up at him suspiciously. "How do we know who?" asked Sara, "and why would someone do this?"

"Someone who has a grudge against me" replied Joe, "and is using Tubby to turn people against me, because people are bound to believe him, and get me removed from the leader position."

The other Chosen Saviours agreed with Joe, and they left the dorm room to look for the truth. They decided to search Tubby's house. If there was indeed an impostor living there, they would find some proof. They hid and waited for Tubby to leave with

Tim keeping guard, and entered Tubby's home to find some clues.

It took them some time, but finally, stuffed in an old cupboard, they found all of the things that were supposed to be missing or stolen by Joe. Just then, Tim whistled as a signal to communicate — Tubby was coming back!

Sara who had stepped inside the cupboard to see better, stepped on something soft and gave a squeal. It was Tubby!

Sara was shocked. Just then the fake Tubby entered and found Sara helping the real Tubby out of the box and the other Chosen Saviours staring at him. He looked aghast! "What are you doing?!" he yelled.

"What are YOU doing?!" Joe asked him "and WHO are you?"

"Joe, Joe" mumbled the real Tubby, "he…… he beat me up and put me in the box. He was going to keep me there forever"

"Nonsense, I never beat you, I only drugged you so that you could stay away, while I got rid of Joe", the fake Tubby prattled off confessing to his own crime in the heat of the moment!

All the Chosen Saviours looked at him in anger, as fake Tubby's eyes grew wide, realizing what he had just done.

With a few more questions, fake Tubby confessed to who he really was. It was the evil trainer who had escaped from prison! The Chosen Saviours quickly tied him up, and waited for the

Saviour police to come and get him. In no time, he was back in prison, this time with chains around his hands and feet.

"But why did he want to get Joe into trouble?" asked Tim, as they sat in the dorm room later with Tubby.

"Because the ex- leader of the saviours was the one who condemned him to 10 years in the saviour offence prison" said Tubby

"But that wasn't Joe" said Jenny.

"It doesn't matter who it was, all that matters to him was that the current leader of the saviours gets punished" said Tubby. "He had a hatred for all the leaders, and wanted revenge one way or another."

"Well, he definitely isn't getting any in prison!" said Jacob, and they all laughed now relieved and hugging Joe with the same warmth as before.

Chapter 8

Joe Gets Hot and Bothered

Joe was not feeling well. He had a bad headache and his body hurt. His stomach was churning and his skin felt unusually hot. "What is happening to me?" he murmured to himself. "Is my body paining because of my morning workout? Is my head aching because of stress? Is my stomach churning because I ate too much? And why am I feeling unusually weak? Oh, I can't worry about it now. I have a lot of work to do."

For Joe, work was more important than anything in the world. Even health and happiness. Even his friends! It didn't matter if he wasn't feeling well, he still was going to make sure that all the saviours were in order and that they were all learning and growing properly.

If only he had taken the trouble to go to the doctor. The doctor would have told him that he had a fever and needed to go to bed at once. But no, Joe was not going to give up on his work just because of some tiny aches and pains. Joe went to work and after a long, hard, tiring day, he went to bed feeling worse than ever.

When Joe woke up, he had big, dark circles under his eyes. He had not slept at all the night before. He was feeling worse than yesterday and to top it all there was a new problem on Earth. The Earth was heating up because of global warming and Joe had to figure out a way to stop it. But he couldn't do it alone. Especially not in his current state. He decided to call Tim and Jenny.

When Tim and Jenny arrived, they were startled seeing Joe's haggard condition.

"Joe! What happened to you in the eight months that we haven't seen you! I thought we told you not to work so hard that you ignore your health!" Jenny cried, running to Joe.

"How about you go to bed and rest so you feel better. We can solve this problem after, or the chosen saviours can take care of it." Tim suggested in worry.

"No. I won't let anyone else do my job. I may be a little unwell but I will be okay soon. I'll come back and rest. The chosen saviours are at a crucial part of training and I don't want to interrupt that for them." Joe said firmly, indicating that was the end of this discussion on his health.

"If you say so. But you know that we'd be happy to help if only you'd just ask." Tim said regretfully and eager to help in whatever way possible.

"I know I know" said Joe feeling physically weak and knowing well they would do all they could to help.

They got to work and started by looking up the definition of global warming on Soogle.

They found out that global warming, also called climate change, is a rise in the temperature of the Earth's climate system. All the effects that happen because of it, like melting polar ice caps, melting glaciers, floods, changing weather, drought and more. Some parts of Earth actually get warmer while some other parts get colder. They also found out that pollution is one of the major causes of climate change, so they decided to go to Earth and try to stop people from polluting the environment.

Once they reached Earth, they saw mounds of garbage and smoke in every city. They landed in Beijing, China, where the smoke was so bad, they were coughing and could barely see.

Beijing is the capital of China and is one of the most developed cities. China itself has a huge population being one of the most industrially developed places, it has tons of factories that give out harmful smoke and gases.

Joe, who was already feeling poorly, started coughing severely because of the smoke. Since he was already feeling weak, he collapsed. Both Tim and Jenny rushed him to the hospital. After running a few tests, and giving Joe some medicines, the doctors told Tim and Jenny that Joe would be fine with some rest.

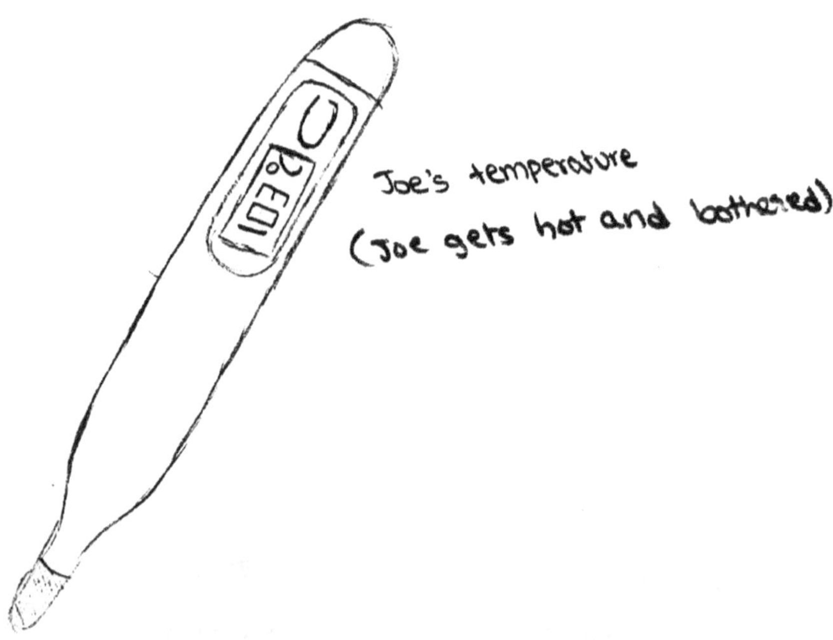

However, the medicines wouldn't work immediately so until they slowly healed him, Joe needed to rest completely. His skin was pale and he had beads of sweat rolling down his body. It felt like there were a thousand needles inside his head that were piercing him inside out. His whole body ached and he felt like retching most of the time. Joe could barely move and had been ordered by the doctor that at any cost he should not get out of bed unless he had a death wish. Yet, despite all of that, Joe wanted to go help the problem he had come to Earth to solve.

Seeing Joe's predicament, Jenny decided to stay in the hospital to look after him and make sure he didn't do anything reckless, while Tim tried to solve the problem. They informed the other saviours about Joe. All of the saviours sent get—well presents for Joe since he was well liked and was their leader. There were bouquets of flowers, boxes of chocolates, books, games, get well soon cards and cakes. Joe felt very nice receiving them, almost like he wasn't unwell anymore.

After a few days Joe left the hospital despite doctor's orders, and Tim and Jenny's advice. Joe was eager to help solve global warming as it was already delayed due to his health. Listening to his protests, they had no choice but to listen to him and have him help them.

The three of them set to work to try and reduce pollution. However they realized it was not so easy to fix. They couldn't just shut down factories or stop cars that emitted smoke. People needed these things. The saviours had saved Earth from monsters, aliens, machines and criminals, but pollution is much harder to cure as there is no specific person to blame. They couldn't punish any one person for this because it is caused by everyone's actions in their day to day life. Usually, the saviours didn't even help with problems like this. They only helped with magic related issues but everyone agreed that their intervention was required in this case.

After brainstorming for several days, Jenny came up with an idea. "We need to make people more aware of climate change and the pollution problem. We can't solve this problem for humans. They have created it and only they can solve it for themselves. We can only show them how, help and motivate them to do it!" she said.

Joe and Tim agreed. "But how?" asked Tim.

"Joe, you will make and put up posters all around the city. Tim, you start a *Save the Environment Campaign* along with the other saviours and I will go to Tubby and see if he can help us out or come up with some more ideas to resolve this problem." she said.

All three agreed this was a great idea and got to work immediately to put the plan in action.

Joe remembered Jimmy, who used to be his friend and classmate in school and just happened to be great at school-projects, to help make posters. Jimmy, who cared a lot about the environment, happily agreed and they got to work.

Tim and the other saviours went around to peoples' homes asking them to join a campaign to stop global warming. They also educated people about what they could do to reduce pollution and save planet Earth for the future generations to come.

Meanwhile, Jenny met Tubby and the rest of the chosen saviours to ask for help. Tubby told Jenny about the Smoke-Eater — a device on the Land of Saviours that would eliminate smoke by eating it. "We can release it towards Earth with a saviour in charge of managing it every morning. This will definitely solve the air pollution problem!" she said "and improve the quality of air".

"Yes" said Tubby. "But this won't solve the problem completely. The real problem is the production of smoke. We need to find a way to stop creating air pollution which only humans can help do." Tubby thought about how environment-friendly the transbocrafts were and suggested that all Earth cars can all be replaced with transbocrafts -- with wheels -- so that they could move on land.

By the end of the week, Joe and Jimmy had put up thousands of posters, Tim's campaign had many members and all the cars and vehicles on Earth were being replaced by transbocrafts.

A few weeks later, Joe used a pollution meter to measure the pollution and find out the measure of impurity in the air. They found it to be much less than before. Everyone cheered and rejoiced. Joe, Jenny and Tim were praised a lot for solving this tough problem.

Chapter 9

Joe's Adventure On A Vacation

Joe had been working very hard as the leader of all the saviours.

He woke up at the crack of dawn, before anyone else had. Made practice schedules for all of the teams. Then after breakfast went to supervise training of all of the teams, correcting them, practising with them and demonstrating the right way to do something when they made a mistake. He was not only a leader to them but their friend too.

Then, post a hurried lunch, Joe went to check on the inmates of the Saviour Offence Prison. Even though Joe had a tough exterior which was needed as a leader, he also had a soft heart that cared for others. However in addition to all this, almost every week Joe had some sort of crazy adventure or a major problem to solve. He was beginning to look tired.

Sara saw how tired Joe looked and suggested that Joe take a break or go on a vacation with her so he could relax and get back the strength and mental alertness that he needed for his work.

"No way" said Joe "I have too much to do" he refused at once without even a thought.

"Tim can take your place for a week" suggested Sara said. Joe thought about it and then considered it, he eventually agreed because he knew that he was overworked mentally and physically and that he would fall ill like the last time. He was overworked and tired and a mission came up.

Tim agreed to stand in for Joe, happy to act as leader for a week, and eager to help his exhausted friend.

Joe and Sara decided to go to Jamaica and started preparing to leave and packing in excitement. After a week of preparing Tim to manage in his absence and preparing themselves with their packing, they left for their vacation.

As soon as they reached Jamaica and got to their hotel, Joe started to unpack but Sara stopped him. "Since we are on a vacation, let's relax first and unpack later" she said. Joe agreed and took a big sigh and smiled.

They went down to the restaurant for a snack after their long journey. Downstairs in the restaurant, the manager recognized them as the Chosen Saviours and greeted them warmly. After their meal, Joe and Sara went to their rooms to relax and unpack. After a while, they decided to go to the beach to relax and enjoy the sun. An hour of relaxation and sun- bathing made them hungry and they sat back and enjoyed some lunch.

"Let's take a look at some of the shops after lunch" suggested Sara. Joe thought it was a good idea as he didn't remember the last time he got a chance to shop. Joe bought himself a souvenir and he bought Sara a lovely little chain with a box which was filled with special sleep sand from the beach. They strolled some more, taking in the sights of Jamaica and getting into the holiday mood. When they got tired, they decided to go back to the hotel.

When they reached the hotel in the evening, it was in total chaos. People were clamouring at the manager, and the manager was looking flustered, while trying to examine something in his hand. Joe asked the manager what was wrong. "Someone has stolen a lot of things and left these notes everywhere" he said, showing Joe the piece of paper in his hand. The note said 'Everyone is Stupid'.

Joe showed Sara the note.

"Don't worry" he said, "we will help you", but Sara stopped him.

"We are on vacation" she reminded him. "I will call my brother Tim" she told the manager. "He will help you as he is standing in as the leader."

Sara and Joe went to their rooms to check if any of their belongings were stolen. She came down after five minutes looking sad and holding a note in her hand. It said, "You are all dumb and I don't think that you immature heroes will catch me". Along with that note there was something else she found.

It was that shell necklace they had bought a few hours ago, which was missing. Sara was surprised that the thief didn't take anything more valuable.

While she and Joe were contemplating the robber's mysterious plan, Tim had reached their hotel in Jamaica. Tim told Sara to make sure Joe does not work due to his fatigue and mentally tiredness. Tim was proud to stand in as leader, even though it was temporary, he wanted to work on this assignment alone. He also did not want Joe to add to his exhaustion by taking up this assignment when he was on a break. Sara took Joe away to distract him and to keep him away from getting involved into it.

That night while everyone was asleep, Tim went to Tubby and asked him to help him with this assignment as he was new to leading and managing an assignment on his own and did not know much about it.

Tubby understood him, as he had also been there himself as a first timer new to an assignment, so together they went to speak to the manager. Tim told the manager that they would like to check the whole hotel to see if they could find any clues that would lead them to the criminal.

Tim and Tubby first went to the storage room because that's where a lot of the spare and valuable stuff was kept in the hotel. When they found nothing there but another mocking note and a few useless stolen things, they started to wonder if this was all just a game for the robber as he/she didn't seem to care about the kind of things they took, or rather stole. In fact, objects with the least value were taken according to Tim and Tubby.

The two of them decided to check the cellar next since they couldn't really go into rooms that visitors were in. They could search the vacant rooms but that wouldn't be of much use because there wouldn't be anything to steal other than the usual furniture and they were sure that even a robber as stupid as the one they were dealing with wouldn't want to steal the room decor when he's left behind precious and expensive items instead.

Again, they only found a note telling them how useless they were when in fact the burglar was the useless one. If you are going to steal, at least do it properly. Or just don't do it at all which is the more sensible and ethically the right option, thought Tubby.

Eventually after all the searching around, Tubby suggested they should search the kitchen because that was the only place left where no notes had been found, nor had any reports come of things being stolen there yet.

As soon as Tubby and Tim walked into the kitchen they saw a glow-in-the-dark, neon green hair band with the letter 'J' embroidered in pink. Tim immediately recognized it as Jenny's. Tim and Tubby went back to the Land of Saviours to question her. As soon as she saw them, she got nervous and confessed to everything.

"I wanted Tim to have an easy problem to solve. He was nervous about being the leader and wasn't confident if he'd know what to do. But he also wanted to do well so badly and prove himself capable. I thought of helping him by creating a fake problem he could resolve and which would make him feel confident and good about himself" confessed Jenny feeling very ashamed of herself.

Tim was embarrassed and angry at first, but forgave her later because he understood her intentions were honourable. He told Joe and Sara about what Jenny did and the reasons behind her doing and they forgave her too.

Jenny went and personally returned all the 'stolen' items belonging to the tourists staying in the hotel. After a week in Jamaica, Joe and Sara travelled back to the Land of Saviours and Joe got back to the job that was most important to him—saving everyone!

Chapter 10

Treasure in the Shipwreck

One beautiful Sunday morning in the land of saviours, news was spreading fast that a ship had been shipwrecked and had sunk to the bottom of the sea.

But what is so important about a ship sinking? It's just a ship after all.

As it happened, a few assigned saviours were travelling aboard this ship and to the royal palace of Solmo, a place which could only be found by those who would look for it.

But that wasn't all.

The saviours were also guarding precious treasure aboard the ship that belonged to the King and Queen of Solmo.

The king had requested the saviours to find the treasure that was stolen from him. The saviours after much difficulty and on giving a tough fight had successfully retrieved it.

They were headed to return it to its rightful owners, which is reigning king and queen of Solmo, when their ship was wrecked due to what looked like a violent storm.

This storm was unlike any and the saviours had reason to believe that rivals of Solmo who were after the treasure had caused it. Thankfully, all the saviours were safe with no-one hurt, but to their disappointment the treasure had sunk.

When the saviours met at Joe's house in the evening, for a friendly get together, Tim and Joe broke this news to them.

"And that is why we have to give it our best shot and try and get back the treasure as fast as we can, before it ends up in the wrong hands" Tim finished.

'What!?' shouted the others in unison.

"Yes, Tubby has given us this new assignment." Tim replied. "Has anybody tried to find the whereabouts of the ship that sank?" he asked Joe.

"Not yet, but it seems the ship sank in a remote part of the sea, that not many others have explored. So other kingdoms would have a hard time finding the ship or the treasure it is carrying" said Joe.

"Even so, there are all kinds of people and some of them will no doubt start looking for it soon enough. Let's not ignore the humans who will send their people to explore the bottom of the sea to look for the sunken ship and its treasure."

"If there are evil people who want to steal the king and queen's treasure hidden in that ship then what are we waiting for? Let's not waste any more time and get working!" shouted Jenny jumping to her feet with excitement.

The saviours packed their diving gear and oxygen tanks and boarded the flight waiting to fly them to the Arabian Sea.

They used a special device moving it above the waters, almost like they were scanning the sea. This device looked like any other simple hand scanner except that it was meant to scan only water bodies for any kind of metal present inside it. The scanner which was black in colour would turn into a bright yellow on detecting any signs of metal on the ocean floor. Which is exactly what happened when they reached the point of the ship wreck.

Once they located the spot, the saviours changed into their dive suits and dove deep into the ocean only to find some other divers looking for the treasure.

Luckily for them, the treasure had been spelled, only the saviours and the royal family of Solmo could see it.

However, the saviours had to act quick and smart to avoid being seen by the other divers, who would definitely start suspecting them.

Joe and the others came up with a plan. Joe would distract the divers while Tim and Andrew would trap them and tie them up. Meanwhile Jenny would search the deck for the treasure and Mathew along with Sara would search the cabins of the ship while Jacob would search around the ship's wreckage.

They put their plan into action. Everyone took their position as planned. Joe bared his teeth and tried to scare the divers. The act was pretty effective as there's not a single person who wouldn't be scared when a vampire pops out of nowhere and comes close to you. He displayed mannerisms showing his intent to kill them.

While Joe surprised the humans, Tim and Andrew trapped them with fishing nets and tied them up. Once all the divers were tied up, Joe swam ahead to help the others while Tim and Andrew stood guarding the other divers.

Mathew was searching the right side of the hull. He found loads of furniture that was rotting due to the sea water. Other than that he found nothing much until he swam to a small hole in the panelling of the ship. He removed that particular panel from the ground, though it took some effort and checking inside for sea creatures. There was something glittering inside that caught his eye. He slipped his hand inside to grab it and managed to get hold of the sacred crown studded with precious jewels that was stolen.

Meanwhile, Sara who was searching the left side of the cabins had found a huge sack of gold coins amongst various supplies and food.

Jenny was searching the top deck and in a corner, hidden under barrels of different things like alcohol, oil and ammunition, had found another sack of coins. It was tied by a rope that was fraying from all sides ready to snap at a moment. Along with the sack of coins was tied an overflowing chest of jewels. Jewels like rubies, emeralds, topaz, diamonds, pearls and yellow sapphire that were of all sizes and shapes glittering and shining like they've just been polished.

Jacob had found some old scrolls protected by magic around the wreckage. They would have been ruined by the water and things that had toppled on top of them in the wreckage, if not for the layer of enchantments and waterproof case wrapped around them.

They all met up on the deck with their findings. Joe checked his list and made sure they had recovered everything. Assured, they came up onto their boat, placed all their finds carefully and sailed off to Solmo to hand over the king's treasure.

The king and queen were so very happy to have the treasure back as they had lost hope of finding it. They rewarded every member of the chosen saviours to choose and take one item they liked most back with them.

Hesitant seeing their generosity but also happy to have earned it with their bravery, the Saviours each picked an item to honour the royals of Solmo. They bid goodbyes and set off on their journey back to their home, The Land of Saviours.

And this is how Joe's super challenging adventure ended.

www.ingramcontent.com/pod-product-compliance
Lightning Source LLC
Chambersburg PA
CBHW051454140726

47987CB00006B/2702